# The Way Between

*The Way Between: A Story of Loss, Listening, and the Quiet Call Home*



*The Way Between* is a work of fiction. Thomas and the other characters in the story are not real people, but elements of their voices and insights were drawn from patients the author has had the privilege of caring for in hospice and end-of-life settings. Names, identifying details, and specific circumstances have been altered or composited to protect the privacy of those individuals and their families.

ISBN: 979-8-234-01672-0

Published by Jerod Hurnblad

Medford, Oregon

# The Way Between

*A Story of Loss, Listening, and the Quiet Call Home*

Jerod Hurnblad

*For everyone who has carried something they didn't choose.*

# Author's Note

My first clear memory is a hospital hallway in Minnesota. I was five. My father was at the Mayo Clinic for a pancreas transplant that hadn't taken, and the family had been told he wouldn't make the night. My mother tried to hurry me past the doorway so I wouldn't see him, but I saw—the machines, the tubes, the beeping, a body that looked like it had already left itself. I cried myself to sleep that night. It was the first thing I understood about being alive: that even the strongest of us, even the ones we can't imagine losing, will one day be held by something bigger than themselves.

My father lived. He lost vision in his right eye a few years later and received a successful kidney transplant when I was ten. My childhood was a map of hospitals—emergency rooms, specialists, waiting rooms where my mother always had snacks in her bag and I colored in books beside her while we waited to see if this cold or that flu would be the one that took him. I grew up with mortality sitting in the room like a quiet guest.

That does something to a child. In my teenage years, I ran from it the way most people run—with substances, with noise, with anything that would turn the volume down. I was nineteen when my middle brother, Jacob Daniel, was killed by a drunk driver in May of 1998. It was a hit and run. The driver was caught.

My father kept saying, before the sentencing, that our family would be known for our love and forgiveness, not our anger. My mother stood up in court and publicly forgave the man who killed her son. She asked for the most lenient sentence the law allowed.

I can't explain what that did to me. I was a young man most of my family had written off—the one they thought would end up in prison or dead. I drove 130,000 miles in my brother's truck over the years that followed, traveling the country, looking for something I couldn't name. The forgiveness I'd witnessed in that courtroom moved slowly through me, the way a stone dropped into deep water keeps falling long after you've stopped watching. It pulled me toward a door I eventually stopped running from. And when I stopped running, a Hand I'd been avoiding my whole life met me there.

My father died of kidney failure in September of 1999, sixteen months after my brother. I helped care for him through his last two weeks of hospice at home. Two months after my father's death, my oldest brother,

Jeremiah, was diagnosed with stage four melanoma and given seven years to live. He survived. He is fifty-three now, and he has been sober for twelve years. I am grateful for him every day.

None of what I have done in the last twenty-two years would have been possible without my wife, Lisa. I met her at a Bible study six months after I got sober. I told her on our first date that I didn't want to kiss her until I married her, and that I wanted to build our life on reading and praying together. She said yes. Our first kiss was at the altar. In every season since—the children we raised, the shifts I came home from still carrying someone else's last breath—she has been the quiet center of our home. She does not always see the strength she carries, but I see it. She is the reason I can do this work. She is the reason I can write this book. She is the person I want beside me at the end of my path, the way the guide walks beside his wife in this story—not because the road has been easy, but because it has sometimes been hard, and we have stayed on it together.

I became a CNA in my forties, though the seed was planted decades earlier—in Minnesota, in the waiting rooms of my childhood, watching nurses care for my father through surgery after surgery. I had talked with

Lisa in our twenties about becoming a nurse. Life didn't line up then. It lined up later, after my stepfather died in 2022, and I was ready.

My mother had a small stroke in 2024, and we moved her close so I could care for her. A year later, she had a larger one. I was working in the emergency room when the call came, and I clocked out and waited for her ambulance to arrive.

She chose comfort care. She had seen enough to know what she wanted. I stayed with her every day on 3 West—my home floor, the oncology and end-of-life unit—while I finished third-semester nursing classes on Zoom beside her bed. The nurses and aides who cared for her were my coworkers. They knew what she needed before she asked. I am forever grateful for the way they held her, and for the way they held me while I was holding her.

On her last day, after my classes had ended, one of the aides—a woman I have worked with from my first day on that floor, who has given over twenty years of her life to caring for the dying—came into my mother's room with tears in her eyes. She walked to the bed, leaned down, and kissed my mother's forehead. "I love you, Vicki," she said. Then she turned to me. She told me she had just been walking down the hallway when she saw something—a vision, she said, of God standing with his arms open wide, saying "welcome home, daughter."

My mother was still breathing that night. I had decided not to fall asleep. I was holding her hand. A song was playing from the speaker by her bed—"O Come to the Altar." When the chorus reached the line "the Father's arms are open wide," she breathed her last.

The welcome had been spoken in the hallway that afternoon. The song echoed it back at the moment it became true.

I did post-mortem care on my own mother. I cleaned her face the way I had cleaned the faces of so many others.

My mother carried depression her whole adult life. It was not a secret. She had been hospitalized for it when I was three, and something deeper broke in her the day my brother was killed. She remarried and loved her family and cared for her children, but the shine never fully came back. For twenty-seven years I watched her live inside a version of herself she couldn't quite reach, with glimmers of the woman she had been surfacing every once in a while before fading into the dark. She always wanted to write a book, but the weight she carried made the small things—the letters unopened, the cards she bought us and never managed to mail—harder than the world knew. This book is, in part, hers. It is what she might have written, if the dark had loosened its grip long enough to let her. Mom, this one is yours.

This book grew out of that room, and many rooms before it.

The characters you've just walked with are not inventions. They are interwoven from people I've been privileged to sit with—patients on my floor who gave me, in their final weeks and sometimes their final hours, wisdom I never asked for and will never be able to repay. A man in his eighties who had buried his wife seven years earlier and told me, after his own terminal diagnosis, that I was living in my golden years right now. A man who spent his life buying old coins hoping the next box would hold the rare one that would make him rich, who told me at the end that his deepest regret was that he had never learned to be content. A man who was terrified at the end of his life and told me his greatest sorrow was that his mother had died before she ever got to meet him clean. The friends I've sat with in recovery rooms across twenty-five years. I have carried their voices from bedside to bedside for a long time. In this book, I've tried to let them speak a little further.

There is one more character whose origin I want to name carefully. The guide Thomas meets on the path is the one I met on mine. I won't say more than that here. Some readers will recognize him. Some will feel a presence in him they can't yet name. Some will simply know that the kind of love the guide offers Thomas—steady, patient, refusing to leave—exists in the world, because they have been met by it somewhere. If the guide becomes familiar to you in the reading, that's not an accident. I wanted him to walk in a story rather than stand behind a pulpit, because I know there are readers who would not trust him if they met him in a church, but might trust him if they met him on a mountain path, beside a fire, on a bench, in the snow.

People sometimes ask how I do this work. How I sit at one bedside after another and still have something to give. The honest answer is that I don't—not really. The longer I've done this, the more clearly I've felt that what moves through me isn't mine. I empty myself into loving people in their hardest moments, and somewhere in that emptying, something fills me back up again. You may hold it differently. You may call it something else, or nothing at all. The book doesn't require you to name it the way I do. But I wanted you to know that for me, the presence that moves through Thomas's story is real. It has a face.

That doesn't mean I don't feel the weight. I take the long way home sometimes. I let the tears come when they come. I don't hurry past what a heavy day leaves in me. I've learned that being present in people's darkest moments is a privilege, not a burden—but only if I let myself feel it honestly rather than pretending to be made of stone.

*The Way Between* is what came of all of this. It is not a roadmap, a resolution, or a promise that the weight eventually lifts. It is a book about moving with grief, and discovering that you were never meant to move alone. It was written slowly, out of seasons where staying mattered more than understanding, and where silence taught more than answers ever could.

If you found yourself lingering in these pages—pausing, remembering, listening—then the story has done what it was meant to do.

Take with you only what remains when the words fall quiet.

The way is closer than it seems. And you are not meant to walk it alone.

— Jerod

# The Leaving

Thomas left without telling anyone it would be for this long.

He told himself it was temporary. A pause. Just enough distance to think. That was the word he used—think—even though thinking was the very thing that had been wearing him thin. What he really wanted was quiet. A kind of quiet that didn't ask questions.

The decision came together the way exhaustion often does: without drama, without clarity, without a clear beginning. One day followed another until something in him reached its limit, and leaving felt easier than staying where everything carried a memory.

The road into the mountains narrowed gradually, almost politely. The air cooled as he climbed, carrying the faint bite of autumn, thinning in a way he felt in his chest before he noticed it in his thoughts. Pines rose first—dark, steady, unchanged—then aspens appeared in widening groves, their leaves already turning, gold catching the light like something briefly aflame.

The contrast struck him.

Evergreen beside surrender. One holding fast, the other letting go without apology.

He hadn't chosen the village for any particular reason. It appeared on the map like an afterthought. No attractions listed. No promises made. That felt right.

By the time he arrived, evening had begun to settle in earlier than he expected, the light withdrawing without explanation. The village didn't announce itself. There was no clear edge where it began, no sense of arrival. Just a quiet gathering of stone buildings shaped by time rather than intention. Roofs sloped gently. Windows were small. Everything looked as though it had learned, long ago, how to endure without needing to be noticed.

Thomas parked near a narrow square where nothing much seemed to happen. Leaves skittered across the stones when the wind passed through, amber and rust against gray. A few lights glowed behind curtains. Somewhere, a door closed. That was all.

The place he was staying sat just above the village center, reached by a footpath worn smooth from years of use. The stones were uneven, softened by weather and repetition, leaves caught in their edges like small, uncollected prayers. The path curved rather than cutting straight up the hill, as if someone had decided effort should be measured, not rushed.

Inside, the room was simple. A bed. A small table. A chair near the window. Thick stone walls held the day's cool, carrying the scent of damp earth and old wood. The quiet here felt different from the quiet he knew at home. It wasn't empty. It felt inhabited.

Thomas set his bag down and sat on the edge of the bed, still wearing his jacket. He didn't move for a while.

Grief, he had learned, didn't always arrive the way people described it. There were no constant tears. No dramatic collapse. It came instead in moments like this—when there was nothing left to do, no one left to perform for, no reason to stay upright.

His brother's name surfaced in his mind, uninvited.

It always did.

Daniel.

He hadn't said it out loud since the funeral. Not because he couldn't, but because speaking it felt like opening a door he wasn't sure he could close again. There were memories attached to the name—shared childhood arguments, inside jokes, a lifetime of knowing someone without explanation. Losing that felt like losing a language no one else spoke.

Thomas leaned forward, elbows on his knees, and let the stillness settle.

Outside, a bell rang.

Not sharply. Not urgently. The sound carried farther in the thinning autumn air—once, then again—unhurried, steady, unconcerned with whether anyone was listening. He had no idea what it marked—time, prayer, habit—but it passed through him all the same.

He exhaled, slower than he had all day.

The bell faded. The quiet returned, thicker now, like fog settling in low places. Thomas didn't know it yet, but this was the first interruption. Not an answer. Not comfort. Just a break in the noise he had been carrying for months.

He stood and crossed to the window.

Below, the village rested in the hollow of the mountain, roofs darkening as dusk deepened. Beyond it, the slope rose into bands of color—aspens glowing gold against the deep green of pines, the whole hillside alive with contrast. Nothing resisted the season. Nothing hurried it along.

Thomas rested his hand against the glass.

He hadn't come here looking for anything. Of that, he was certain. He had come to get away—from the questions, from the well-meaning concern, from the weight of being the one who was still standing.

But standing there now, watching the light drain from the leaves, he felt something else stir beneath the grief. Not hope. Not understanding.

Just the faint sense that he had arrived somewhere he hadn't planned to be.

And that something—someone—was already waiting.

# Thinner Air

By morning, the cold had settled in more firmly.

Thomas noticed it first when he stepped outside, the air sharp enough to wake him fully. His breath showed for a moment, then disappeared. The sky was clear, the kind of blue that only appeared at elevation, clean and unsentimental.

He walked without direction.

It struck him then how little was required of him here. No one asked what he did for a living. No one asked how he was holding up. No one tried to fill the silence.

He walked until his legs warmed and his thoughts began to slow. The village fell behind him, replaced by slope and color and the quiet rhythm of his steps on stone.

Thomas stopped where the path bent sharply, overlooking the slope below. A few leaves broke free from the canopy and drifted down, turning as they fell, untroubled by where they would land.

He watched them longer than necessary.

Something in him recognized the gesture.

He didn't name it. He didn't need to. For the first time since his brother's death, he wasn't trying to carry anything forward or push it away. He was just standing, breathing, allowing the season to be what it was.

The air felt thinner here—not fragile, just honest.

And without realizing it, Thomas slowed his pace, matching the mountain's unhurried way of being.

The path continued on.

So did he.

# The One Who Didn't Ask

Thomas noticed him before he noticed Thomas.

The man was seated on a low stone wall just beyond where the footpath narrowed, a place where the trail paused as if unsure which way to continue. He wore a dark coat, worn at the cuffs, and held a small paper cup between his hands, steam rising faintly into the cold air. Nothing about him stood out. That, Thomas realized, was why he noticed him at all.

He slowed as he approached, unsure whether to pass without acknowledging him. The man looked up, eyes steady, unhurried, as if he had been watching the path long before Thomas came into view.

"Morning," the man said.

It wasn't a question.

"Morning," Thomas replied, surprised by how long it had been since he'd spoken aloud.

The man nodded once, then looked back out over the slope, the colors deepening in the late light. For a moment, neither of them spoke. The silence wasn't awkward. It felt shared.

"Cold comes quicker up here," the man said finally. "Catches people by surprise."

Thomas glanced at his breath, still visible. "Yeah," he said. "It does."

Another pause.

"You're not from here," the man said—not as an observation meant to gather information, but as something gently stated and released.

"No," Thomas said. "Just... visiting."

The man nodded again, as if that answered everything worth asking.

They stood together for a moment longer. Thomas noticed the man didn't look at him directly now, didn't study his face for clues. He seemed content simply to stand beside him, both of them facing the same view.

"That path," the man said, gesturing with his chin, "will take you higher. Not faster. Just... higher."

Thomas followed the gesture. The trail curved upward, disappearing into a stand of trees already shedding their leaves.

"Does it loop back?" Thomas asked.

The man smiled faintly. "Eventually."

That was all he said.

Thomas waited, expecting more—an explanation, a story, some local advice. None came. The man took a sip from his cup, then set it carefully on the stone beside him, as if there were no rush.

After a moment, Thomas realized something unexpected: he felt no urge to fill the silence.

That hadn't happened in a long time.

"I should keep going," Thomas said, more to acknowledge the moment than to end it.

The man nodded, as if he had already known Thomas would.

As Thomas stepped past him, the man spoke again—not louder, not urgent.

"Walk slow," he said. "The ground tells the truth when you give it time."

Thomas stopped, turned back.

But the man was already looking away, his attention returned to the valley below, as if the exchange had concluded the moment it was meant to.

Thomas stood there for a beat longer, then continued up the path.

He didn't try to interpret what had been said. He didn't need to. The words didn't feel like advice. They felt like permission.

Behind him, the village bells rang again—fainter now, carried thinly through the autumn air.

Thomas adjusted his pace without thinking, slowing until his steps matched the rhythm of his breath.

The path rose steadily ahead.

And for the first time since arriving, he didn't feel alone on it.

# What the Mountain Returned

Thomas didn't see the man again that day.

Still, the encounter followed him. Not the words exactly. He couldn't have repeated them if asked. What lingered instead was the absence of demand. The man hadn't asked where he was from, what had brought him there, how long he planned to stay. He hadn't asked the question everyone else eventually asked.

What happened?

Thomas had grown used to preparing for that question, even when it wasn't spoken. His body learned to brace before his mind caught up. A tightening in the chest. A quiet readiness to explain, soften, reassure—I'm okay, really—whether it was true or not.

But on the mountain, nothing had been required of him.

He walked again the next morning, and the morning after that. Always the same path at first, then gradually higher. The season was deepening. Leaves had begun to collect more heavily along the trail, gold and copper pressed into the stone by passing feet.

It occurred to him, with a trace of discomfort, that the mountain had not changed.

He had.

At a bend in the path, he stopped and sat on a low outcropping, the rock cool even through his jacket. Below him, the village lay quiet, smoke lifting from one chimney and then another as evening approached.

He thought of his brother—not sharply this time, not as an interruption, but as a presence that arrived and stayed. The memories came differently here. They did not demand reaction. They simply appeared, like the leaves falling one by one—unavoidable, but not violent.

He realized then how much effort he had spent, for months, trying to manage his grief. To understand it. Contain it. Make it acceptable to others and survivable for himself.

Up here, there was no one to manage it for.

The mountain did not look away. It did not lean in. It simply remained.

For the first time since the loss, Thomas wondered what it would be like not to carry his grief as something that needed explanation.

The thought frightened him.

If he didn't explain it—if he didn't name it—what would be left of him?

&

A single snowflake landed on his sleeve.

Then another.

They were small, almost tentative, dissolving as soon as they touched the warmth of his coat. The aspens trembled faintly as the flakes drifted through them, white passing briefly through gold before falling out of sight. Above him, snow had begun to settle into the branches, bending them low, each limb carrying what it could without complaint.

Thomas watched as a branch released its load all at once. Snow slid free and fell soundlessly to the ground, the limb springing back into place—lighter, unburdened, still standing.

The man stood nearby, his back turned, hands clasped loosely behind him. He didn't turn when Thomas approached.

Thomas stopped a short distance away and stood beside him, both of them facing the same slope, the same fire of color fading gently into dusk.

Neither spoke.

“Fall doesn’t resist,” he said quietly. “It just lets go when it’s time.”

Thomas felt the words land—not as instruction, but as recognition.

The man turned then, just enough to meet Thomas’s eyes. There was no assessment there. No expectation. Only something like understanding, offered and released in the same breath.

Then he nodded once and walked on, his steps unhurried, disappearing around the bend where the path thinned and dropped out of sight.

As Thomas descended toward the village, the light retreating into the deeper blues of evening, he noticed the man from the path below him on a narrow trail that branched toward the far edge of the village.

He was not alone.

A woman walked beside him—slowly, carefully, her steps small and uncertain. The man held her hand. Not the way someone leads another person. The way someone says I’m still here.

Thomas slowed without meaning to.

The woman did not look up. Her head was lowered, her gaze fixed somewhere beneath the path, beneath the snow, beneath whatever the world had become for her.

The man adjusted his pace to match hers, each step measured, unhurried, as if he had walked this exact route at this exact speed a thousand times before.

His thumb moved once across the back of her hand.

Thomas looked away. Not because it was wrong to see. Because it felt like standing at the threshold of something sacred—something he hadn't earned the right to enter.

He continued down the path, the image settling into him the way the mountain's silence had—without explanation, without instruction.

Just something witnessed. Something he would carry without knowing yet what it meant.

He breathed in slowly.

And for the first time, he did not try to hold himself together.

He simply stood.

The mountain held the rest.

# The Place It Broke Open

The emotion came without warning.

Thomas had stopped beneath a cluster of pines where the path widened briefly, the ground layered with needles and fallen leaves dampened by the faint snow. The flurry had already passed, leaving behind nothing more than a suggestion—cold air, darker soil, a sheen on stone.

He stood there, hands in his pockets, thinking of nothing in particular.

And then his chest tightened.

Not sharply. Not violently. Just enough to steal the rhythm from his breath.

He leaned forward slightly, instinctively bracing, waiting for the familiar sequence to follow—the surge of memory, the pressure to contain it, the quiet command to get through this. That was how it usually worked. Emotion arrived as something to be managed.

But this time, nothing followed.

No image. No sentence. No clear thought.

Just the weight.

Thomas bent at the waist, resting his hands on his knees, breath shallow now. The cold seeped through his jacket. A few flakes, late and indecisive, drifted down and vanished against the dark ground.

His throat tightened.

He swallowed, once, then again.

The sound that escaped him surprised him—not a sob, not a cry, but something lower, almost animal, pulled from somewhere beneath language. It came out in a breath he hadn't planned to release.

He straightened instinctively, glancing around, half-expecting someone to be there.

No one was.

The path lay empty in both directions. The mountain stood as it always had—bare branches overhead, stone indifferent to his posture.

Thomas's shoulders shook once.

Then again.

He lowered himself onto the ground, back against the trunk of a pine, the needles sharp through his coat. He didn't fight it this time. Didn't try to quiet himself or translate the feeling into something safer.

Tears came—not in a rush, but steadily, as if they had been waiting for permission. They tracked down his face, warm against the cold, disappearing into the collar of his jacket.

He thought of his brother—not the hospital, not the phone call, not the finality of it all—but of a moment years earlier, standing side by side in a place not unlike this, neither of them speaking, both content simply to be there. Daniel squinting into the sun the way he always did when he was thinking something through. That particular squint—not the face from the end, which Thomas had spent months trying to unlearn, but this one. The one that said he was still present. Still here. Still himself.

And then another memory arrived behind it—a night at Daniel's apartment, a box of old basketball cards spread across the floor between them. Thomas had held one up, half-joking, and Daniel told him the player's college without looking. So Thomas held up another. Same thing. Another. Same thing. They went through the whole box, Thomas laughing harder each time, Daniel never once wrong, never reaching for his phone, just knowing—the way some people carry facts the way others carry songs, effortlessly, without purpose, as if the information had chosen him. Thomas couldn't remember what they'd been drinking, or what year it was, or why they'd pulled the box out in the first place. But he remembered the laughter. And that no one at the funeral would have known to mention it.

Thomas pressed his forehead briefly against his hands and let the grief move through him—not as an enemy, not as something to overcome, but as something that had earned its right to be felt.

The mountain did not recoil.

Wind moved through the aspens, shaking loose a scatter of leaves that fell among the pine needles, their color muted now, almost bronze. Somewhere above him, snow brushed the higher ridges, invisible from where he sat.

Time stretched.

Eventually, his breathing slowed. The tightness eased—not gone, but softened, like ground after the first frost. Thomas wiped his face with the sleeve of his jacket and leaned back against the tree, staring up through the branches at the pale sky.

He felt emptied.

And strangely, steadied.

For the first time since the loss, he understood that grief was not asking to be solved. It was asking to be allowed.

He didn't thank the mountain. Didn't pray. Didn't promise anything in return.

He simply stayed until the cold reminded him he was still a body in a season that was changing.

When he stood, his legs stiff, the path ahead looked the same as it had before.

But Thomas walked it differently.

Slower. Unprotected. Listening—not for answers, but for what remained when he stopped resisting.

Above him, unseen, snow continued to gather where the mountain rose higher—quietly preparing the ground for something not yet revealed.

# The Locked Door

Thomas noticed the church because it was always quiet.

Not abandoned—there were signs of care in the stonework, the roof kept whole, the narrow windows clear—but closed in a way that felt intentional. It sat just off one of the upper paths, its walls darkened by weather, its door set back beneath a shallow arch worn smooth by centuries of hands that no longer came.

He passed it the first time without stopping. The second time, he slowed. By the third morning, he turned off the path deliberately and stood before it, breath fogging in the cold air.

The door was solid wood, thick and scarred, iron fittings dark with age. No hours posted. No explanation offered. He tried the handle once, gently. It held fast.

The refusal was so ordinary it almost embarrassed him.

He stood there longer than the moment required, hand still resting on the cold iron, surprised by the sting of it. He had not come looking for sanctuary. Not exactly. He had come because the building was quiet, because the path kept bringing him past it, because some part of him still believed that if a door this old existed, it ought to open for people carrying what he was carrying.

But it didn't.

And the ache that rose in him had very little to do with the church.

He thought, briefly, of all the doors he had stood before in the past year—hospital rooms, offices, quiet homes filled with people trying not to say the wrong thing. Doors that had opened and delivered news he hadn't been ready to receive.

This one stayed closed.

Thomas sat on the low stone step beneath the arch, his back against the cold wall. The stone pressed firmly between his shoulders, grounding him.

He realized then how much effort he had spent believing that access was proof of worth. That open doors meant approval. That if something remained closed, it was because he hadn't done enough, hadn't asked correctly, hadn't been faithful in the right way.

The door did not correct him. It did not invite him in. It simply remained.

And somehow, sitting there without entry, Thomas felt less rejected than he had in months.

He felt—unexpectedly—held.

❧

He returned the next morning.

Snow had changed the path overnight, softening its edges. The church appeared the same. Stone darkened by cold. The arch worn smooth. The door closed.

Thomas didn't reach for the handle. He simply sat on the step again, hands in his pockets, and let the ache arrive without rushing to resolve it.

A thought surfaced—not fully formed, more like a pressure than a sentence.

What if the door isn't closed to keep you out?

He didn't answer it.

Another followed.

What if it's closed so you stop mistaking entry for presence?

Thomas opened his eyes. He felt no disappointment. Instead, there was a strange steadiness—an awareness that whatever he was seeking did not require access to a room, or permission from a threshold.

He stood slowly. Before turning away, he placed his hand flat against the door—not to open it, not to test it, but simply to feel its solidity beneath his palm. The wood was cold, unmoving, real.

He left his hand there for a moment longer than necessary.

Then he stepped back.

As he turned toward the path, he noticed something he hadn't before: a narrow trail branching away from the church, almost hidden beneath snow and leaves. It didn't lead anywhere obvious.

The church did not call him inside. The path did not announce itself either.

But one invited movement.

He followed it.

Behind him, the door remained closed—unchanged, unoffended, patient.

And for the first time, Thomas did not feel that he was leaving something behind. He felt that he was being led—without explanation, without guarantee—into whatever came next.

# What Was Shared

The smell reached him first.

Wood smoke—rich, layered, carrying something else beneath it. Bread, maybe. Or stew. The kind of scent that didn't advertise itself but assumed you knew what it meant.

The path widened into a small clearing where several buildings leaned toward one another. Light spilled from low windows, golden and steady. The sound of voices drifted through the air—not loud, but threaded with familiarity.

Thomas stopped just short of the clearing, uncertain whether he was meant to continue. The instinct to retreat surfaced quickly—polite, automatic, well-trained.

A woman glanced up briefly from where she was setting bowls on the table. She didn't smile. She didn't frown. She simply nodded, once, as if acknowledging something already understood.

"Cold night," she said, turning back to her work.

Someone handed him a bowl. No ceremony. No explanation.

He took it without thinking.

The stew was thick, dark with root vegetables and herbs. He found a place at the table where no one asked him to introduce himself. Conversation flowed around him—short exchanges, shared observations about weather, wood supply, the coming frost. Nothing personal. Nothing guarded.

Across the table, he noticed the man from the path. He was seated slightly apart, not isolated, just unassuming—hands resting around a cup, gaze directed toward the fire.

Thomas felt something loosen inside him.

Not joy. Not relief.

Belonging.

Not the kind that demands history or explanation. The kind that arrives when no one asks you to justify your presence.

When the bowls were empty, Thomas rose and carried his to where the others were stacking them. No one thanked him. He washed it alongside someone he didn't know, the water cold, his hands steady.

As the group dispersed, the man from the path paused at the edge of the clearing.

"Storm'll come tonight," he said quietly. "Nothing heavy. Just enough to cover what's already fallen."

Thomas nodded. The man stepped into the dark and was gone.

Thomas lingered a moment longer, then turned back toward the path. He realized then that no one had asked him why he was there.

And for the first time, he didn't feel the need to answer.

# Nightfall

Night came quickly.

The snow thickened as Thomas walked, not heavy enough to blind him, but steady enough to change the sound of the mountain. The hush deepened, the kind that absorbs rather than echoes. His steps softened beneath him, each one landing quieter than the last.

He hadn't meant to be out this long.

The trail behind the church had led him farther than expected, winding gently through trees that now stood dark and indistinct against the sky. What had felt clear in daylight became uncertain as dusk dissolved the edges of things.

Thomas stopped.

The world narrowed to what his breath could reach.

He listened.

Wind moved through the pines above him, steady and low. Snow brushed against his jacket, against his face, melting and returning as cold. Somewhere nearby, water moved beneath ice, its sound faint but certain.

For the first time since arriving, uncertainty pressed in—not emotional this time, but practical.

He turned slowly, trying to recognize the bend in the trail he had passed minutes earlier. Everything looked the same. Snow erased the distinction between path and ground, invitation and boundary.

A familiar instinct rose—tight, urgent.

Figure this out. Move faster. Don't stop.

Instead, Thomas stood still.

He thought of the man's words from days earlier. Walk slow.

He exhaled and let his shoulders drop.

Then he saw the light.

It was faint at first, just a soft amber glow filtering through the trees downslope. It didn't move. It didn't call attention to itself. It simply remained, patient against the dark.

Thomas adjusted his direction and followed it carefully, step by measured step. The light grew clearer as he descended, resolving into the window of a small building set slightly apart from the others, smoke rising thinly from its chimney.

He approached without urgency now.

A door opened before he reached it.

The woman from the clearing stood there, wrapped in a thick shawl, her hair pulled back loosely. She didn't look surprised to see him.

"The mountain doesn't lose people," she said. "It just waits until they stop."

Thomas nodded. "I lost the trail."

She stepped aside. "Come in."

Inside, warmth wrapped around him immediately. A fire burned low in the hearth, its light moving gently across the stone walls. A few others sat nearby—quiet, unhurried, as if night had settled into the room long before it arrived outside.

No one asked where he had been.

Someone handed him a cup. Tea this time. Bitter and grounding.

Thomas sat near the fire, boots drying, snow melting onto the stone floor beneath him. His hands warmed slowly around the cup. The tension he hadn't realized he was holding eased.

&

The fire crackled low. The others in the room moved with the quiet rhythm of people who had long since stopped needing to fill silence with sound. Someone added a log.

Someone else adjusted a lamp. The gestures were small, practiced, and without performance.

Thomas recognized the woman—the same one who had set bowls on the table the first evening, who had nodded him into the clearing without ceremony.

She sat across from him now, her shawl drawn loosely around her shoulders, both hands resting against a cup she hadn't touched. She watched the fire the way someone watches the ocean—not for movement, but for steadiness.

After a long while, she spoke. Not to Thomas specifically. To the room. To whoever was ready to hear it.

"He was the kind of man who made plans," she said.

No one stirred. The others didn't react. They had heard this before. They simply held the space the way the village had taught them to.

"We were married forty-one years," she continued. "Not all of them easy. But all of them ours. We had plans—real ones, the kind you write down and tape to the refrigerator so you see them every morning. Travel the country. Visit the grandchildren more. Buy a motorhome—we'd already taken one trip in it. He drove the whole way and wouldn't let me touch the radio."

A faint smile crossed her face. It didn't stay.

"And then the diagnosis came."

She said it plainly. The way someone names a season.

"Cancer. Early, they said. But it didn't stay early."

Thomas felt the room shift. Not in sound—in weight. The air thickened the way it does when someone begins to carry something out loud that they've been carrying alone.

"I cried," she said. "For weeks, I cried. And then I stopped crying and started doing. Because that's what you do when the person you love is disappearing in front of you. You don't sit with it. You move. You make calls. You drive to appointments. You learn words you never wanted to learn."

She paused. Her thumb moved slowly across the rim of her cup.

"And then the appointments stop. And the driving stops. And the words stop mattering because the body has already decided."

Thomas did not move.

"I bathed him," she said. "Every day. I brushed his teeth. I combed his hair even after he stopped knowing it was me doing it. I watched the man I adored slip away from me piece by piece—first his strength, then his voice, then the look in his eyes that told me he knew who I was."

Her voice did not break. It had been rebuilt too many times for that. It held the way the stone walls of the church held—cracked in places, weathered everywhere, still standing.

"At the end, we were hand in hand," she said. "His breathing changed. Got slower. Farther apart. I held on and I talked to him even though I don't know if he heard me. And then he stopped."

Silence held the room. The fire popped once. A log settled.

The others did not look at her. Not out of discomfort. Out of respect. They had each sat where she was sitting. They knew the weight of the chair.

"When he passed," she said, "I asked them to let me stay. The nurses, the caretakers. I asked if I could be the one to clean him. To prepare his body. They weren't sure at first. But I told them—I had bathed him every day for the last year of his life. I wasn't going to stop now."

Thomas felt his throat close. She had done it herself. Not because it was her job. Not because anyone expected it. Because it was her devotion.

"I washed him one last time," she said. "Combed his hair. Buttoned his shirt—the good one, the one he wore on our first trip in the motorhome. And I sat with him after. Not because anyone told me to. Because I wasn't finished loving him yet."

Thomas's eyes grew heavy. He did not try to stop it.

The woman looked at him then. Not through him. At him. The way someone looks at a person who is younger than they realize and older than they know.

"We had all these plans," she said. "The trips. The grandchildren. The golden years—that's what we called them. We were going to live them when he retired. When the timing was right. When everything lined up."

She set her cup down.

"The timing never lined up. And the golden years never came. Not the ones we imagined."

She leaned forward slightly, and when she spoke, her voice carried something that was not grief and not wisdom but something between them—the hard-won clarity of someone who paid full price for what she knows.

"You're living in your golden years right now," she said. "Don't think that waiting is going to make them better. Live your life."

The words landed in the room and no one moved to pick them up. They just sat there, glowing, the way embers do after the flame has passed.

Thomas looked at the fire. He thought of Daniel—not the loss of him, but the life of him. The walks. The laughter that came easily. The way he never seemed to be saving himself for later. He had lived as if now was all he'd been given. And he'd been right.

Night pressed against the windows, thick and complete.

And for the first time since arriving, Thomas allowed himself to be guided without knowing where it would lead.

# What Staying Asks

Morning arrived muted.

Snow lay clean and even across the village, smoothing edges, quieting color. The trees stood stripped and patient, their branches holding what the sky had given them.

Near the edge of the square, Thomas saw the man from the path. He stood alone, brushing snow from the bench with his glove, methodical, unhurried.

"Paths'll open again by afternoon," the man said. "If that's what you're waiting for."

"I wasn't," Thomas said.

Silence settled between them, companionable but weighted.

"I should head back soon," Thomas added, surprising himself. The words felt practiced, familiar—the kind he'd used before leaving home. Temporary. Responsible. Safe.

The man finally looked at him then.

"Maybe," he said. "But leaving's easy."

Thomas felt the truth of it immediately. Leaving meant relief. Leaving meant forward motion that looked like progress. Staying meant uncertainty. It meant carrying grief without armor.

The man turned away, the conversation complete.

❧

Thomas packed his bag the way someone does when they aren't sure they're leaving.

He zipped it partway. Then stopped.

He stood and crossed to the window. The morning light caught the bare branches differently now—stark against the white ground, each one visible in a way they hadn't been when the leaves were full.

Thomas reached for his jacket. He left the bag where it was.

The path led him down toward the square. The man stood near a stack of firewood, splitting logs with steady, practiced rhythm. He didn't look up as Thomas approached.

The man paused between swings, straightened slowly, and pressed the heel of his hand against his lower back. It lasted only a moment—a small negotiation with something that had been there a long time. Then he set the next log and continued.

"You've got time?" the man asked, adjusting the wood without breaking cadence.

Thomas hesitated. "I think so."

The man handed him the axe. No ceremony. No explanation.

Thomas took it, feeling its weight settle into his hands. He positioned the log, raised the axe, and brought it down—not cleanly, but enough. The wood cracked and separated.

They worked without speaking, the rhythm forming naturally. Strike. Reset. Stack.

After a while, the man spoke. "We'll need more before night. Storms come heavier later in the season."

Thomas wiped his hands on his jacket. "I can help."

The words settled between them, unremarkable and irreversible all at once.

"That'd be good," the man said.

Thomas realized then that he had made a choice without announcing it.

He stayed.

# What Was Asked

The request came later, when the light had begun to fade again.

Thomas had spent the afternoon helping where he was needed—carrying supplies, clearing snow from steps, holding doors without being told. No one thanked him. No one questioned his presence. The work spoke for itself.

As evening settled, he found the man near the edge of the village, standing beside a narrow shed tucked against the slope. The wind pressed harder now, colder, carrying the promise of another storm.

"There's a trail above here," the man said, gesturing toward the darkening line of trees. "Short walk. Steep."

Thomas nodded.

"An older man lives up there," the man continued. "Keeps to himself. Doesn't come down much once the snow starts."

He paused, letting the information rest without instruction.

"He'll need wood," the man said finally. "Before the path closes for good."

Thomas waited.

"Someone usually brings it," the man added. "This year, that someone isn't here."

The wind moved through the aspens above them, branches knocking softly against one another. Snow drifted down, sparse but persistent.

Thomas understood the request now.

It wasn't symbolic. It wasn't optional. It wasn't framed as kindness.

It was simply something that needed doing.

"I can take it," Thomas said.

The man studied him for a moment longer than usual—not measuring, but noticing. Then he nodded.

"Tomorrow morning," he said. "Before the light goes."

Thomas looked toward the trail. It was already darkening, the incline sharp, the snow uneven.

"Alright," he said.

The man turned away, the matter settled.

Thomas stood there alone for a moment, the weight of the decision settling in. Staying now meant responsibility. It meant effort without recognition. It meant walking uphill into cold and uncertainty for someone he had never met.

He felt the familiar flicker of resistance.

Then he felt something else—quieter, steadier.

Purpose, unadorned.

Not because it healed anything. Not because it proved anything.

Because it was asked.

Thomas pulled his jacket tighter and headed back toward the warmth of the village, snow gathering on his shoulders again. Above him, the mountain loomed, darker now, patient and sure.

For the first time, staying felt less like avoidance and more like obedience—though he did not yet have words for what he was obeying.

Only that he would walk the trail in the morning.

And that, for now, was enough.

# The Weight of the Ascent

Thomas started before the light fully arrived.

The village lay muted beneath a low gray sky. He adjusted the straps on the pack, the weight of the bundled wood settling across his shoulders heavier than he expected. Not unbearable—just enough to make the climb matter.

The trail narrowed quickly as it rose. His boots sank deeper than they had the day before, each step requiring more attention.

He hadn't gone far before his breath shortened.

The trees closed in around him, their branches interlocking overhead, the canopy thinner now but no less present. Branches bowed low beneath the weight of snow, some nearly brushing the ground, their patience a kind of instruction Thomas hadn't asked for.

A clump of snow dropped from above and landed at his feet, heavy and sudden. The silence that followed felt louder than the sound.

Halfway up, the thought surfaced clearly for the first time:

You don't have to do this.

It arrived calmly, reasonably. He could turn back. No one would be angry. The village would manage.

Thomas stopped. He leaned against the trunk of a pine, the rough bark pressing through his jacket, grounding him. He imagined setting the pack down. Walking back empty-handed, breath easing with each step downhill.

The image brought immediate relief.

And then—just as quickly—something tightened.

He thought of the locked church—the door unmoving, uninterested in persuasion. How it had asked nothing of him except honesty. He thought of the firelight, how it had gathered strangers without explanation. He thought of the man handing him the axe—trust placed quietly in his hands.

And he thought of Daniel. Not the squint this time. Not the laugh. But the way his brother used to walk—always a half-step ahead, not from impatience but from eagerness, as if the world perpetually held something worth getting to. Thomas had spent a year trying to outrun the loss of that. Up here, he understood, for the first time, that he had only ever been walking toward it.

This wasn't about the wood.

It was about how long he had lived braced against weight he was never meant to carry alone.

Thomas bent and adjusted the pack, tightening the straps, letting the weight settle where it belonged. When he straightened, the path ahead had not changed.

But he had.

He took the next step. Then another. His pace slowed, deliberate now, matched to his breath.

At a bend in the trail, the trees opened briefly, revealing the slope below. The village appeared smaller from here, softened by distance and snow, chimneys drawing thin lines against the gray sky.

Thomas paused only long enough to breathe.

Then he turned back to the path and continued upward.

# The Waiting Place

No one answered when Thomas knocked.

The sound landed solidly against the wood and disappeared into the quiet. He waited, listening for movement from inside—footsteps, a shift of weight, anything that might suggest he had been heard.

Nothing came.

Thomas glanced back down the trail. Snow had begun to fall again, finer this time, drifting sideways on the wind. The path he had climbed was already softening, his tracks losing definition.

He knocked again, gentler now.

Still nothing.

He shifted his weight, feeling the ache in his legs settle deeper, the cold pressing more insistently through his jacket. The effort of the climb had kept him warm; standing still invited the mountain back in.

Thomas stepped back from the door and set the pack of wood down carefully beneath the small overhang. He rubbed his hands together, breath quickening slightly as the cold crept in.

The waiting stretched.

Minutes passed—maybe longer. Time thinned here, unmarked by anything but breath and snowfall. He thought briefly of turning back, of returning with the explanation that no one had answered. It would be true. It would be enough.

But something held him there.

Not resolve. Not determination.

Just the quiet sense that leaving now would feel unfinished.

Thomas leaned against the cabin wall, the wood rough beneath his shoulder, and let the cold settle into him. Snow gathered on the brim of his jacket, on his boots, on the bundle at his feet. The mountain did not rush him. It simply waited alongside him.

He noticed then how quiet his thoughts had become.

No rehearsed explanations. No internal defense. No bargaining.

Just presence.

When the door finally opened, it did so without warning.

The man who stood there was older than Thomas had expected—lean, weathered, his hair white and uncombed, his face marked by lines that spoke more of endurance than age. He squinted slightly against the light, as if he had been sitting in the dark for a long time.

They regarded one another in silence.

"You're early," the man said finally.

Thomas almost smiled. "I thought I was late."

The man looked at the sky, the snow, the wood at Thomas's feet. He nodded once.

"Cold waits for no one," he said.

He stepped aside.

Inside, the cabin was dim but warm. A woodstove ticked in the corner, its iron sides radiating heat that pressed back the cold in waves. The walls were lined with shelves and tools worn smooth by use. The air smelled of resin and something older—time, maybe. Or solitude.

Thomas carried the wood in without being asked, stacking it neatly beside the hearth. The motion felt natural, expected. When he finished, he straightened, flexing his fingers.

The older man watched him quietly.

"You came all the way up here," he said. Not a question.

Thomas nodded. "I was asked."

The man grunted softly, as if that were explanation enough.

He reached for a jar on the shelf and unscrewed the lid. The smell of dried herbs filled the small space—sharp, medicinal, not unpleasant. He pinched a measure into a dented tin mug and poured water from a pot already warm on the hearth. He set it near Thomas without comment, then gestured toward a small stool.

"Sit," he said.

Thomas obeyed, grateful for the heat now pressing back the cold in his bones. Snow melted from his jacket and dripped quietly onto the stone floor.

Thomas took the mug. The heat pressed through the tin into his palms, sharp and immediate.

They sat in silence for a while, the fire crackling softly between them.

❧

"You waiting for something?" the man asked eventually.

Thomas considered the question.

"I didn't think I was," he said.

The man nodded. "Most aren't."

He leaned back slightly, studying Thomas with eyes that did not pry, did not evaluate. They simply rested there, steady and unafraid.

Then, without ceremony, the man spoke.

"I had a family once," he said. "Parents who loved me in the way people do when they don't know how to say it—through meals kept warm, doors left unlocked, arguments that ended in silence because the love was bigger than the words."

Thomas did not move.

"I lost someone," the man continued. "Doesn't matter who. What matters is what I did with the loss."

He stared into the fire. The light moved across his face, catching the lines, the hollows, the places where time had pressed hardest.

"I ran," he said simply. "Not with my legs. With everything I could find to put between me and the feeling. At first it worked. Whatever I reached for dulled the ache just enough to let me breathe. And I told myself that was surviving."

Thomas felt the words settle into his chest. He recognized the shape of them—not the specifics, but the architecture. The reaching. The relief. The reaching again.

The man's voice lowered. He looked at the fire as if reading something written in it.

"I wrote something once," he said. "During the worst of it. When I was still inside. I still remember the words."

He was quiet for a moment. Then he spoke them, and his voice changed—younger, rawer, the voice of the man he had been.

"Somehow these old musings don't satisfy or quiet the ache. The attempt to dull just doesn't allow the escape from all this feeling. Empty and alone, not sure where to turn. But turning away to escape the thoughts and feelings of such deep loss only increases the emptiness."

He paused. The fire popped once. A log shifted and settled.

"What once allowed the escape is taking its own grip. What once offered solace is now stealing who I am."

The words hung in the cabin—present tense, still alive, still burning even though the man who wrote them had made it to the other side.

His voice returned to his own—older, steadier, rougher.

"I reached for whatever substance could dull the ache," he said. "And eventually it stole the loss from me. I couldn't even feel the original wound anymore. But I was still running. Only now I wasn't running from the loss. I was running from the person I had become."

The words landed in the cabin like something set down after being carried too long.

Thomas did not speak. He understood now that this was not a lesson being taught. It was a confession being offered.

The man looked at him.

"The thing you think is the escape," he said, "becomes the coffin. You climb inside it willingly because it feels like shelter. And by the time you realize what it is, the lid is already closing."

Thomas felt his breath catch.

"And while you're inside it," the man continued, "you can't see what's happening. You point outward. Everyone else is the problem. The world is wrong, the people around you don't understand, they're too demanding, too close, too much. That projection—that blame—isn't you. It's the thing holding on tighter. Because the moment you stop pointing out there and look in here—"

He pressed a hand against his chest.

"—the whole illusion falls apart."

Silence held the room.

The man stared at the fire for a long time. When he spoke again, his voice carried something different—not anger, but the weariness of someone who has been misunderstood for so long he stopped expecting otherwise.

"The world looks at an addict and sees a choice," he said. "Just stop. As if willpower could overpower a pain you can't even name. As if choosing sobriety is as simple as choosing a different shirt. No one chooses addiction. They choose relief. And by the time the relief becomes the prison, the choice is gone."

He leaned forward.

"The substance was never the problem. It was the answer to a problem no one bothered to ask about. The wound came first—the grief, the trauma, the loss—and the substance was the only language I had for surviving it. But the world doesn't see the wound. It sees the behavior. It treats the symptom and wonders why the disease keeps coming back."

Thomas thought of the people he had known who carried things they never named. The ones who smiled the widest. The ones who deflected with humor. The ones who seemed fine.

"And then the shame," the man said quietly. "The world shames you for the very thing you're drowning in. And you swallow the shame because you believe you deserve it. And the shame becomes another wound that needs numbing. And the numbing drives more use. And the use creates more shame. A spiral with no bottom and no exit—because the very thing meant to save you, the judgment, the intervention, the love withdrawn as leverage—it tightens the grip."

The man went quiet. He wrapped both hands around the mug and looked into it, as though the next words hadn't arrived yet.

He looked at Thomas.

"The person inside the addiction is still a person," he said. "Still someone's son. Still someone's brother. The addiction doesn't replace them. It buries them. And the work of recovery isn't becoming someone new. It's digging yourself out and finding that the person you were is still there—underneath everything you piled on top of him to survive."

"My parents watched it happen," he said. His voice did not break. It had been broken long before and mended into something rougher. "They watched their son disappear while he was still standing in front of them. I was alive. I was breathing. I was in their house, at their table, looking at them with eyes they didn't recognize. And they grieved me. They mourned a living person."

Thomas felt his throat tighten. He thought of the people who had watched him retreat after Daniel died—

the careful distance, the well-meaning concern, the doors he had closed without slamming them.

"They died before I got clean," the man said.

The sentence arrived without drama. Without performance. Just the plain, unrecoverable fact of it.

"They never saw who I actually was underneath all of it. They carried the grief of losing me their entire lives. And I carry the grief of never being known by them. Not really. Not the way I am now."

He looked at the fire.

"That's a loss that runs both directions," he said. "They lost me while I was alive. And I lost them before I was awake enough to know what I had."

Thomas's hands stilled in his lap. His chest was not as steady.

A log collapsed in the stove, sending a brief flare of light across the walls. The man watched it settle. Neither of them moved to replace it.

The man leaned forward slightly, not toward Thomas, but toward the fire, toward the warmth, toward whatever he was still learning to sit with.

"The hardship has to be faced," he said. "The sorrow. The tragedy. Not tomorrow. Not when you're ready. Not when you've found the right strategy or the right words or the right person to hold your hand through it. Now. Because every day you turn away from it, the emptiness gets bigger. And whatever you're using to fill it gets hungrier."

He sat back.

"Sitting with the feeling," he said. "That's where the healing begins. Not past it. Not through it. In it. The thought of loss, the weight of it, the thing you've been running from—it's still there. It was always there. Running just gave it time to grow roots."

Thomas looked at the man—really looked at him. The white hair. The worn hands. The face that had weathered more than cold. And he saw it now: not wisdom earned by reflection, but wisdom earned by destitution. The kind that only comes after you've lost everything, including yourself, and had to rebuild from whatever was left.

"How did you stop?" Thomas asked. His voice was quiet. He wasn't sure he had the right to ask.

The man was quiet for a long time. When he spoke, his voice was different. Lower. Rougher. The voice of someone going back to a room he doesn't visit often.

"There was a night," he said.

He didn't look at Thomas. He looked at the fire, but Thomas could tell he wasn't seeing it.

"The darkest one. Not the worst thing that had happened to me—I'd had plenty of those. But the emptiest. I was alone. Whatever I'd used that night had stopped working hours before, and the ache was louder than it had ever been. Not screaming. Worse than screaming. Just—present. Filling the room. Filling me. And there was nothing left to put between me and it."

His hands trembled slightly. He clasped them together, not to hide it, but to hold himself steady.

"And in that silence," he said, "I saw two doors."

Thomas did not breathe.

"One was the door I'd been walking through for years. Let the thing finish what it started. Stop fighting. Stop pretending there was something left worth saving. Just—go quiet. The way a fire goes out when no one feeds it."

He swallowed. The sound was audible in the still room.

"The other door was unthinkable. The other door was turning around and facing everything I'd been running from. Every feeling I'd buried. Every memory I'd drowned. Every piece of myself I'd handed over to the thing that promised it would carry the weight for me."

He looked at Thomas now. His eyes were wet. He did not wipe them.

"That door was the fight," he said. "Not against the substance. Against the demons underneath it. The grief I never let myself feel. The shame I never sat with. The voice inside that said I wasn't strong enough to survive my own pain without something to numb it."

Thomas felt his own eyes burn. He held still.

"I chose the fight," the man said.

He let the words stand alone for a moment.

"People don't understand what that means," he said. "They think getting clean is quitting something. Like putting down a bad habit. It's not. Getting clean is volunteering to feel every single thing you've spent years making sure you never felt. Every wound. Every memory. Every shame. Every loss. It all comes rushing back the moment the numbing stops. There's no easing into it. There's no halfway. You're dropped into hostile territory inside your own body—no extraction, no timeline, no guarantee you survive it."

His voice was steady now. Not calm—hardened. The steadiness of a man describing a war he fought alone.

"The strength it takes to do that—to sit in a room, shaking, choosing to stay conscious for one more hour—

no one sees it. There's no medal. No recognition. Just a person at war with themselves, choosing every single day not to reach for the thing that made the pain stop. And doing it again the next day. And the next. For years."

He looked at his hands.

"That's the loneliest fight there is," he said. "Not because you're alone in the room—but because the world has already decided what you are. And when the world has made up its mind about you, your war becomes invisible. You're fighting for your life and no one in the room believes you're worth saving—including yourself."

Thomas sat with the weight of it. The silence between them was not empty. It was sacred.

"But I need you to understand something," the man said. "I didn't do it alone."

He unclasped his hands and placed them flat on his knees.

"That night—the darkest one—when I saw the two doors, I had nothing left. No strength. No will. No reason to choose the harder one. Everything in me had already surrendered. And yet something refused to let the story end in that room."

His voice dropped to almost a whisper.

"I said I didn't know what it was. I said I didn't have a name for it. But I do."

He looked at Thomas.

"It was a hand," he said. "Reaching through the dark. Not waiting until I was clean. Not waiting until I deserved it. Reaching into the pit while I was still in it—filthy, broken, barely breathing—and refusing to let go. A grace I didn't earn, didn't ask for, and couldn't have survived without."

Thomas felt something move through him that was not grief and not relief but something older than both.

"The fight was mine," the man said. "Every hour of it. Every shaking, sleepless, white-knuckled hour. But the flicker that started the fight—the refusal to die in that room—that wasn't me. That was something that loved me before I could love myself. Something that saw someone valuable buried beneath everything I'd become—and decided I was worth pulling out."

He was quiet for a moment.

"I came back the way the prodigal comes back," he said. "Not cleaned up. Not worthy. Covered in everything I'd done to myself. And the hand was still there. It never left. It was just waiting for me to stop running long enough to feel it."

The room held what he had said. Snow ticked against the window. Thomas let his breath slow.

“The demons don’t die,” he said. “I want you to know that. You don’t slay them. You don’t outrun them. You face them. You stand in the room with them and you refuse to leave. And slowly—not all at once, not cleanly—they lose their grip. Not because you’re stronger. Because you stopped feeding them the one thing they needed to survive.”

“Which was?” Thomas asked.

“Your silence,” the man said. “Your refusal to look at what happened. As long as I kept the feelings detached from the events that caused them, they roamed free. Like a sickness with no source. I couldn’t trace the pain back to anything because I’d buried the connection so deep. And so the feelings just—moved through me. Unnamed. Unattached. Pulling me under.”

He paused.

“But when I finally sat with it—when I stopped running and let the feeling lead me back to the wound—something shifted. I learned to reframe what had happened to me. Not change it. The events don’t change. The loss doesn’t undo itself. The years don’t come back. But in the reframing, I began to shape my own response to it. I began to realize I wasn't a passenger in my own grief. That I had a say in what it meant—not what it took from me, but what it taught me."

He looked at Thomas with something that was not quite peace and not quite sorrow. Something earned.

"That's the freedom," he said. "Not freedom from the pain. Freedom inside it. The realization that you are actually in control. That you get to shape how you feel. Not by avoiding it. Not by numbing it. By sitting with it long enough to understand what it's asking of you."

The fire crackled. Snow pressed against the window.

Thomas sat with the weight of everything the man had given him. He didn't try to organize it or respond to it or make it fit into something manageable. He just let it be there.

The man watched him do it. And something in his face—something old and tired and unguarded—softened.

"You're here," he said quietly. "That's not nothing."

☙

When Thomas finally stood to leave, the snow had lightened, the storm easing as quietly as it had arrived. He pulled on his jacket, the warmth lingering beneath it now.

At the door, he paused.

“Thank you,” he said—not for the shelter, not for the warmth, but for the thing the man had set down between them that Thomas would carry differently now.

The man inclined his head slightly.

“Walk slow,” he said. “Winter teaches best when you listen.”

Thomas stepped back into the cold, the door closing softly behind him.

The mountain received him again, snow-muted and sure.

He began the descent carefully, the weight on his shoulders gone now, replaced by something lighter, steadier—an understanding that waiting had not been wasted time.

It had been the work.

# What He Carried Down

The descent took longer than Thomas expected.

Not because the path was difficult—though snow had softened its edges again—but because he moved differently now. More carefully. More attentively. Each step placed with intention, as if the mountain required consent rather than momentum.

The cabin disappeared behind him quickly, swallowed by trees and falling snow. Nothing marked the place except the faint disturbance where his boots had pressed into the path. Within minutes, even that began to fade.

He hadn't taken anything with him.

No words to repeat. No instruction to follow. No explanation to bring back.

And yet, something had shifted.

The waiting lingered in him—not as frustration, but as a steadiness he hadn't known before. He realized he was no longer scanning his thoughts for meaning, no longer rehearsing what the encounter had been about. It existed now the way warmth does after leaving a fire—unseen, but undeniable.

Snow dropped from the canopy as he passed, landing in soft bursts around his boots. The trees let go of what they'd been holding the way the mountain let go of everything—without ceremony.

Thomas stopped once, mid-descent.

Not because he was tired.

Because he felt full.

The grief was still there. He could feel it—steady, present, no longer demanding attention. It walked with him now instead of pulling at him from behind. And for the first time, he did not try to outrun it.

By the time the village came into view, the light had shifted again. Late afternoon softened the edges of everything, chimneys visible now against the fading light, the sound of life returning gently to his awareness.

Thomas stepped onto the lower path and felt the difference immediately.

He was carrying less.

And he hadn't lost anything.

# When He Was Seen

The man was waiting near the bench by the square.

Not sitting. Not pacing. Just standing, hands tucked into his coat, gaze resting on the mountains as if they were continuing a conversation that hadn't needed words in the first place.

Thomas slowed instinctively.

The man didn't turn right away. He spoke without looking at him.

"You made it up."

Thomas nodded. "And back."

The man glanced at him then—briefly, carefully. Something passed between them that felt less like evaluation and more like acknowledgment.

"Good," he said.

They stood together for a moment, the village quiet around them. Snowmelt dripped from eaves. Somewhere, wood was being split again, the sound sharp and rhythmic against the cold air.

"You didn't hurry down," the man added.

It wasn't a question.

Thomas hadn't realized it until that moment. He looked at his boots, damp with snow, the evidence of his pace pressed into their seams.

"No," he said. "I didn't."

The man nodded once, satisfied.

"That'll matter," he said.

Silence returned, comfortable now, familiar. Thomas felt no urge to fill it. The man didn't offer anything else—no praise, no commentary, no summary of what the day had meant.

After a moment, he gestured toward the village.

"They'll be setting the fire again tonight," he said. "Storm's still a day out."

Thomas followed his gaze. The clearing already showed signs of preparation—wood stacked higher, a few people moving with quiet efficiency.

"I can help," Thomas said.

The man smiled faintly—not approval, not encouragement. Recognition.

"I figured you would."

They turned together and began walking, their steps naturally falling into rhythm.

As they walked, Thomas noticed something he hadn't before—a thin cord around the man's wrist, nearly hidden beneath his sleeve. Worn smooth, frayed at the edges, the kind of thing that had been tied there so long it had become part of the skin beneath it.

Thomas didn't ask.

The man noticed him noticing.

He was quiet for several steps. Then, without looking down at it, he said:

"My daughter made it."

The words arrived simply. No weight placed on them. No invitation to respond.

"She was seven," he said. "She made it from a piece of string she found in the yard. Tied it on my wrist herself. Told me it was so I'd always know where home was."

Thomas felt something shift in the air between them. Not heavier. Just more honest.

"She was killed," the man said. "A car accident. No warning. No preparation. One morning she was at the table asking for more syrup on her pancakes. By that evening she was gone."

The path continued beneath them. Snow crunched softly. The village stretched quiet around them, smoke rising in thin threads from the houses nearest the square.

Thomas did not speak. He understood that this was not a door being opened for discussion. It was a fact being set down between them—solid, unalterable, carried for so long it had worn smooth like the cord on his wrist.

The man looked at the mountains.

"She would have liked it here," he said. "She liked snow."

Then he continued walking, and Thomas walked beside him, and neither of them spoke again until the path widened and the village received them back into its quiet rhythm.

Thomas understood then that the man walking beside him did not lead the way from wisdom alone.

He led from wreckage.

# When Winter Stayed

Winter did not arrive all at once.

It settled in quietly, almost politely, as if testing whether anyone would object. Snow fell in thinner, steadier layers. Paths narrowed. Sounds softened. The village adjusted without complaint.

Thomas learned the rhythm quickly.

Morning fires were lit earlier. Water was drawn with more care. Work that had once been scattered across the day now clustered around the brief hours of light. No one spoke of inconvenience. They simply adapted.

He did the same.

His days filled with small, necessary tasks—splitting wood, clearing steps, carrying supplies uphill and back again. The work asked for his body more than his thoughts, and he welcomed that. Hunger came honestly now. Sleep arrived without argument.

The mountain pressed closer.

Aspens stood bare, their branches pale against the sky, rattling softly when the wind moved through them. Pines bore the weight of snow in thick layers, bending slightly but holding fast. Thomas found himself watching how they differed—how neither resisted what the season demanded.

The locked church disappeared beneath snow, its door half-buried now, the arch outlined in white. Thomas passed it without stopping.

Not because it no longer mattered. Because it did not need to be revisited.

Evenings gathered people together more often. Fires burned longer. Meals stretched, unhurried, punctuated by shared silence rather than conversation. Thomas noticed how little anyone explained themselves. Life here was shaped by presence, not narrative.

And slowly—without announcement—this became his life.

The grief remained, but it had changed shape. It no longer flared unexpectedly. It moved with him now, quieter, heavier in some ways, but no longer sharp. Like the snow, it had settled into everything rather than interrupting it.

One night, as Thomas stood outside after the fire had burned low, he looked up at the mountain rising dark and complete against the sky. He thought of his brother—not with the sharp pull he had come to expect, but gently, the way you think of someone who is simply elsewhere. As if

Daniel were standing just outside the circle of light, watching the same sky.

Thomas did not try to hold the feeling or explain it.

He realized winter had stayed.

And so had he.

One evening, as the light drained from the sky earlier than it had the day before, Thomas saw them again.

The man and the woman. Walking the same narrow trail at the edge of the village. The same pace. The same hand holding hers. The same small, patient steps.

But this time Thomas was closer.

He could see her face.

It was not the face of someone walking. It was the face of someone being walked. Her eyes were open but unfocused, resting on something far beyond the path, beyond the snow, beyond anything Thomas could see. Her expression held no pain. No sadness. Nothing. The absence itself was the wound—a vacancy where a person had once been.

The guide spoke to her softly as they moved. Thomas couldn't hear the words. But he could see the man's lips moving, steady, gentle, the way someone reads aloud to a child who may already be asleep. Not because they'll hear it. Because the reading itself is the love.

Thomas stood still until they passed out of sight.

His chest ached in a way he hadn't felt since the early days. Not for himself. For the man who had been guiding him all this time—who had handed him the axe, sent him up the mountain—carrying this. Every day. Without once letting it show.

&

He found the man later, near the bench by the square. Alone now. Sitting for the first time Thomas could remember.

Thomas sat beside him without asking.

The silence held for a long time. Snow fell lightly. The village dimmed.

Finally, Thomas spoke.

"The woman you walk with," he said carefully. "Who is she?"

The man didn't answer right away. His hands rested on his knees. His breath rose and disappeared.

"My wife," he said.

The word carried everything.

Thomas waited.

"When our daughter was killed," the man said, "my wife couldn't find her way back. The grief swallowed her whole. Not all at once—slowly. The way winter takes a river. First the edges freeze. Then the surface. Then everything beneath it goes still."

He looked at the sky.

"She's still in there," he said. "I know she is. Because every once in a while—maybe once a month, maybe less—I get a glimmer. She'll look at me and I'll see her. Really see her. The woman I married. The woman who laughed so hard she couldn't breathe. And then she fades back into the dark, and I'm holding the hand of someone who barely knows I'm there."

Thomas felt his jaw tighten. He did not trust himself to speak.

"I bathe her," the man said. "When she can't get herself out of bed. When life is too heavy for her to lift her own arms. I wash her hair. I dress her. I talk to her even when her eyes are somewhere else. Because the covenant I made wasn't for the good days. It was for all of them."

Here was a man whose wife had lost everything, including herself, and he had stayed. Not because she asked. Because he promised.

"Anyone can love when life is kind," the man said quietly. "When the house is full and the days are easy and the person beside you is whole. That's not the test. The test is whether you love when it costs you everything. When the person you gave your life for can't give anything back. When staying means choosing pain over relief, every single day, with no guarantee that it will ever be returned."

He looked at his hands—the same hands that dressed his wife that morning, that held hers on the trail, that once held his daughter.

"Love isn't a feeling that happens to you," he said. "It's a choice. And what makes it sacred is that it's given when it costs everything—and the one giving it chose freely."

Thomas felt the shape of something press against the walls of his understanding—something larger than the man beside him, larger than the bench and the snow and the village. A truth so old it had no author.

The man leaned forward, elbows on his knees.

"People ask me how I do it," he said. "How I wake up every morning and care for someone who barely sees me. How I don't feel cheated. How I'm not angry."

He paused.

"I was angry," he said. "For a long time. At the driver who killed my daughter. At God for not protecting her. At myself for not being there—as if my body between her and the car could have changed anything. Three kinds of unforgiveness, all living in the same chest."

He pressed a hand flat against his sternum.

"Unforgiveness toward the one who took her. Unforgiveness toward God for allowing it. And the most sinister one of all—the inability to forgive myself."

Thomas felt the words land like stones dropped into deep water.

He sat back.

"I stood before the man who killed my daughter," he said. "And I forgave him."

The sentence hung in the cold air.

"Not because he deserved it. Not because the anger was gone. Because I understood that holding it was costing me the only thing I had left—my ability to love what remained."

Thomas exhaled. He hadn't realized he'd been holding his breath.

"And then I had to forgive God," the man said. "Which is harder than people think. Because forgiving God means accepting that He didn't intervene. That the protection I prayed for didn't come in the form I asked for. And sitting with that—with a God who is good and a world that is broken—that's the hardest room to be in."

He looked at Thomas.

"And then I had to forgive myself. Which is the room most people never enter. Because forgiving yourself means admitting you couldn't control it. That your love wasn't enough to stop it. That being a good father didn't protect her from the world."

Thomas felt something crack open in his chest. He thought of Daniel. Not the loss—the guilt. The quiet, corrosive belief that he should have done more, been more, seen something coming that no one could have seen. The guilt that wore the mask of grief but was really just the unbearable weight of being the one who survived.

The man watched him. And Thomas knew, without either of them saying it, that the guide had seen that weight in him from the very first morning on the path.

Thomas opened his mouth. Closed it. Opened it again.

The words had been sitting in him for months—longer—pressed down beneath everything else, beneath the grief and the silence and the careful way he had learned to talk about his brother without ever saying how.

"He took his own life," Thomas said.

The words left him like something released from a cage. Not loud. Not dramatic. Just the fact of it, finally, in the open air.

The man did not flinch. Did not shift. Did not look away.

Thomas felt his hands shaking. He pressed them against his knees.

"No one knows what to do with it," he said. His voice was thick, unsteady, unfamiliar to him. "When someone dies of cancer, people know the script. They bring food. They say the right things. When someone takes their own life, the room changes. People look at you differently. They don't say the wrong thing—they say nothing. And the nothing is worse."

The guide listened. The fire crackled between them.

"He was the most alive person I knew," Thomas continued. "The squint into the sun. The laugh that came from nowhere. The walks when things felt tangled. He seemed—fine. More than fine. He seemed like the one who had it figured out."

His voice broke. He let it.

"And every one of those memories is evidence now. Every laugh I took at face value. Every 'I'm fine' I accepted because it was easier than pressing. Every time he deflected and I let him, because the performance was convincing and I wanted to believe it."

Thomas pressed his palms against his eyes.

"I should have known," he said. "I was his brother. I sat across from him a hundred times and I never saw it. Or I saw it and I looked away. And I'll never know which one is true, and that's the thing I can't put down."

The silence that followed was not empty. It was full—full of everything Thomas had just set down between them, everything he had been carrying since before the first page of this story began.

The man let it sit. He did not rush to fill it. He did not offer comfort or explanation or Scripture. He sat with Thomas the way the mountain sat with snow—receiving it, holding it, letting it rest where it fell.

After a long time, the man spoke.

"Your brother's pain," he said carefully, "was bigger than his ability to carry it. That is not your failure. That is not something your love could have fixed. You could have seen every sign and pressed every time and sat in every silence, and his pain would still have been his."

Thomas's shoulders shook once. Then again.

"Loving someone," the man said, "does not give you the power to save them. It gives you the power to be present with them. And you were. He knew that. Even if his pain was louder."

Thomas wept. Not the way he had on the mountain—not the sudden, animal release of grief held too long. This was different. This was the weeping of a man who had just spoken the unspeakable and found that the ground did not open beneath him. That the person beside him did not leave. That the word he had been carrying like a stone in his chest had finally been set down, and the world was still here.

The man placed his hand on Thomas's shoulder. He did not squeeze. He did not pull him close. He simply rested it there—steady, warm, present.

And Thomas let himself be held by it.

"Gratitude," the man said quietly, "is the only thing that saved me."

He let the word sit.

"Not happiness. Not understanding. Gratitude. The deliberate, daily choice to remember what I was given rather than what was taken. The day my wife found out she was pregnant—the look on her face, the way her hands went to her stomach before her mind caught up. Seven years with a daughter who made every room she walked into feel warmer. The day I met my wife—what seemed like an ordinary afternoon that turned out to be the beginning of everything."

His voice steadied.

"The laughs. The warm glances. The quiet words we said to each other that no one else heard. What seemed insignificant at the time—those are the memories I hold closest now. Because they were real. And they were mine. And no accident, no diagnosis, no amount of darkness can take them from me."

Thomas sat with it. All of it. The daughter. The wife. The forgiveness. The gratitude. The man beside him who had lost more than anyone Thomas had ever met and had chosen—every single day—to hold the light instead of the dark.

"Regret is not a room to dwell in," the man said. "If you choose it, it becomes a cell you can't escape. Regret has its place—it teaches you to appreciate what you have when you have it. But if you move in, if you furnish it and make it home, it will hold you prisoner."

Snow fell between them. The village settled into its evening quiet. Somewhere a door closed softly. Somewhere else, a fire was lit.

Thomas did not move for a long time.

He sat beside the man who had guided him through every season of this place—fall's letting go, winter's dark night, and now, faintly, the first whisper of something that might become spring. And he understood that the guide had not been teaching him how to survive grief.

He had been showing him how to live inside it. With gratitude. With forgiveness. With hands open and a heart that refused to close.

# What Was Asked of Him

The man found him the next morning near the edge of the square.

Snow fell lightly again, almost habitually now, as if the mountain had settled into a pattern it saw no reason to change. The man stood with his hands clasped behind his back, his breath rising in slow, steady clouds.

"You've been here long enough," he said.

It wasn't a dismissal. It was an observation.

Thomas nodded. "I know."

They stood in silence for a moment, watching someone haul water across the packed snow, their steps careful but practiced.

"There's something we don't ask often," the man said finally.

Thomas felt the words land before he understood them.

"When winter closes in like this," the man continued, "some people don't come down anymore. Not because they can't. Because they won't."

Thomas turned to look at him.

“There’s a woman,” the man said. “Lives farther along the ridge. Her husband left. Keeps to herself.”

He paused.

"She hasn't been seen in weeks."

The familiar structure of the request did not follow.

No task. No distance measured. No instructions given.

Instead, the man looked at Thomas fully now.

"She doesn't need wood," he said. "She doesn't need food. Others have taken care of that."

Thomas waited.

"She needs someone to sit," the man finished. "Someone who won't try to fix anything."

The cost revealed itself immediately.

This was not carrying weight uphill. Not splitting wood. Not braving weather.

This was presence.

Thomas felt his chest tighten—not with fear, but with recognition. He knew this terrain. He had spent months avoiding it. Sitting with someone else's grief meant allowing his own to remain uncovered.

"I don't know what to say," Thomas said quietly.

The man nodded. "Good."

Silence stretched between them, deeper than before.

"She won't thank you," the man added. "She may not even speak."

Thomas thought of the locked church. The closed door. The waiting. The firelight. The old man in the cabin. The way grief had changed when it was allowed to exist without correction.

He exhaled slowly.

"When?" he asked.

The man inclined his head toward the ridge. "Today. While the path's still passable."

Thomas looked toward the mountain, white and patient, its slopes heavier now, its demands quieter but more insistent.

This was different.

Staying had been easy once winter took hold. Helping had followed naturally. But this—this asked him to step directly into the place he had been learning to inhabit without protection.

He nodded.

"I'll go," he said.

The man did not smile.

He simply turned and walked away, the matter settled.

Thomas stood there for a moment longer, snow gathering lightly on his shoulders.

Then he turned toward the ridge and began to walk—knowing that this time, the weight he carried would not be visible.

And that it would matter more because of it.

# The Borrowed Room

The path to her home was less traveled.

Snow lay deeper here, undisturbed except for a narrow line where someone had passed days ago—maybe longer. Thomas followed it carefully, his steps slower now, more deliberate. The mountain felt quieter on this side of the ridge, the trees closer together, the sky lower.

The climb was gentler than the one he had made before, but the weight felt different.

He wasn't carrying anything in his hands.

That made it harder.

The woman's home sat near the edge of the ridge, partially sheltered by a stand of pines whose branches bowed low with snow. A thin line of smoke rose from the chimney. The windows were dim.

Thomas stopped a short distance away.

The instinct to turn back surfaced quickly this time—not out of fear, but respect. He did not want to intrude. He did not want to arrive with the wrong posture, the wrong words, the wrong hope.

He stood there, letting the cold settle, letting the silence speak first.

Then he walked on.

The door was simple. Unpainted. Worn by weather and time. He knocked once, lightly, then waited.

Nothing.

He knocked again, softer still.

This time, he heard movement—slow, careful, as if each step required negotiation. The door opened only a few inches.

The woman's face appeared in the gap, her eyes wary but not unkind. Her hair was pulled back loosely, streaked with gray, her features drawn in a way Thomas recognized immediately—not from age, but from the particular weariness of someone who had stopped expecting company.

"Yes?" she said.

"I was asked to come," Thomas replied. He didn't mention who had asked. It didn't seem necessary.

The door opened wider.

She studied him for a moment longer than comfort allowed, then stepped aside without a word.

Inside, the air was cool but not cold. A small fire burned low in the hearth, its light dim, as if conserving itself. The room was spare—functional rather than empty. A table. Two chairs. A shelf lined with jars and dried herbs. On the far wall, a single photograph in a wooden frame, its glass catching what little light the lamp offered.

Thomas removed his jacket and stood, unsure at first where to place himself.

She gestured toward a chair.

He sat.

For a long while, neither of them spoke. The silence here felt heavier than the quiet he had grown accustomed to—dense, layered, shaped by absence.

Eventually, the woman spoke.

“No one has sat in that chair,” she said, nodding toward the one Thomas occupied. “Not since I came here.”

Thomas did not shift in the seat. He let the weight of what she had said settle over him without moving away from it.

He noticed then that the cabin held two of everything. Two chairs. Two cups on the shelf. Two hooks by the door. The habits of a life built alongside someone, carried into a place where she was alone.

She did not explain.

He did not ask.

She rose without a word, moved to the stove, and returned with a folded cloth and a small bowl of broth. She placed it at the edge of the table near his side—close enough to reach, not pushed toward him. The distinction felt important.

Thomas wrapped his hands around the bowl. The heat pressed into his palms.

Time passed. The lamp flickered once, held.

❧

When she finally spoke again, her voice was quieter. Not fragile. Measured. The voice of someone who had rehearsed something so many times it no longer needed rehearsal.

“We were young when we found each other,” she said. “We had nothing. Not nothing the way people say it when they mean they had less—I mean nothing. A borrowed room. One set of dishes. A coat we shared because we couldn’t afford two.”

She looked toward the window, though there was nothing to see beyond the frost.

“He worked. I don’t mean he had a job—I mean he worked the way some men do when they believe that building something will prove they deserve what they’ve been given. He climbed. Every rung, every title, every room with a longer table and a heavier door. And I was beside him for all of it."

Thomas did not speak. Something in her voice held him still—not its sadness, but its steadiness. The way it carried the full weight without shaking.

"We traveled the world," she continued. "Places I had only read about in books I borrowed from the library because we couldn't buy them. And then we could buy them. And then we could buy the shelf they sat on, and the house that held the shelf, and another house after that."

"We went to Pompeii once," she said. "Walked through the ruins. You could see where the tables had been. Where the bread was left. Where people were sitting when it all ended. An entire city that had everything—wealth, beauty, life in full motion—gone in a single day. And all that was left were the outlines. The shapes of what had been."

She looked at Thomas.

"I walked through it and thought how sad. How sudden. I didn't understand yet that I was looking at my own life."

"We never wanted for anything."

The words carried no bitterness. No longing. They arrived the way facts do—steady, certain, stripped of their former warmth.

Thomas waited.

"But all of it—the gold, the silver, the places, the things—none of it had substance without the person I shared it with."

Her voice caught. Not much. Just enough to show that the surface she had built over the years was thinner than it appeared.

She placed the bowl aside, both hands flat on the table, steadying herself the way a person does when the ground shifts beneath something they thought was settled.

"When he left, everything lost its shine. Gold and silver were no longer brilliant. They faded to a dull tan and gray. I stood in the same rooms, wore the same things, looked out the same windows. But the color had gone out of all of it."

Thomas felt his chest tighten. He recognized the geography she was describing—the world unchanged yet unrecognizable. The way loss reshapes a room without moving a single piece of furniture.

She looked at him then—not for comfort, not for confirmation. She looked at him the way someone looks at a witness. To see if they are still there.

He was.

"He left me for something shinier," she said. The words did not tremble. They had been carried too long for that. "A younger version. A prettier version. Someone who still reflected back to him the man he wanted to believe he was."

She exhaled slowly.

"And with her, he kept climbing. Kept chasing the illusion. The next room, the next title, the next proof that he was enough."

"All the chasing," she said quietly, "was wrapped up in the same illusion. Only to find emptiness at the end of it. And then the urge to fill it again. Another pursuit, another promise, another thing that was supposed to be the answer. And when it wasn't, the emptiness came back louder than before."

She looked down at her hands.

"An endless loop," she said. "One that can only end in regret. Because the thing you're chasing was never out there. And by the time you realize that, you've already left behind everything that was real."

Silence settled again. Snow ticked faintly against the window.

"What he never understood," she said, "was that the depth of what we had wasn't built in the gold years. It was built in the borrowed room. It was formed in the hardships. In the disagreements. In the nights we turned away from each other and the mornings we chose to turn back."

Her voice steadied further, as if arriving somewhere she had walked to many times before.

"The love wasn't made in the having. It was made in the making up."

Thomas felt something give way inside him—not dramatically, not all at once, but the way a frozen stream begins to move beneath the surface before the ice above it shows any sign of cracking.

He thought of Daniel. Not the squint this time. Not the laugh. But the way his brother used to sit across from him at a kitchen table not unlike this one, saying nothing, comfortable in the quiet the way only people who have argued and forgiven can be.

His eyes burned. He did not look away.

The woman watched him, and something in her face softened—not pity, never that—but the recognition of someone who understood that tears held back take up more room than tears released.

"I ran the same loop," she said after a moment. "After he left. I redecorated rooms no one visited. Traveled to places that meant nothing without someone to share them with. Stayed busy the way people do when they're afraid of what the stillness will say."

She paused.

"And every time I reached the end of whatever I was chasing, the emptiness was waiting. Patient. Unchanged. As if it had never left."

Thomas recognized the pattern. He had lived inside it without naming it.

"It took losing everything," she said, "for the room to finally empty. The wealth. The house. The life I'd built on top of something I couldn't see. All of it, gone. And when there was nothing left—when the gold had faded and the shine had gone and I was sitting alone in a room not unlike the one we started in—I looked down."

She placed her hands flat on the table.

"And contentment was right there. Beneath my feet. It had always been there. I just couldn't see it while I was running."

The word settled into the room the way a quiet snow begins—so soft you almost miss it, until you notice everything has changed.

"Not happiness," she said. "Not peace. Contentment. The willingness to be where you are with what you have, and to stop believing that the next thing will be the thing that finally makes you whole."

She looked around the cabin—the spare walls, the low fire, the single photograph, the two chairs.

"I wasn't able to learn it while I had everything," she said. "The loss was the teacher. I had to lose it all to find what was always within reach."

Thomas let his hands fall to his knees. They were not steady.

"My brother was like that," he said quietly. His voice was thicker than he expected. "Daniel. He didn't chase. He just—stayed. Wherever he was, he was there. Fully. Even when things were heavy, he didn't try to fix it or fill it with something. He'd just make space for it. Let it be there without needing it to be anything else."

She looked at him with the calm attention of someone recognizing a shared language.

"Yes," she said softly. "Space."

A faint smile crossed her face, brief but real.

Neither of them moved to fill the quiet that followed. It didn't need filling. That was the point—allowing the loss to be there without reaching for something to cover it. Not an external thing. Not an internal lack. Just the willingness to let it exist without asking it to leave.

They sat together as the light shifted and the room grew quieter. No more stories followed. No details exchanged beyond what had already been given.

Thomas realized then that when two people build a life together, they create something between them that belongs to neither one alone. A third thing. An identity that lives only in the space where they meet. And when that ends—whether by death or by leaving—that thing dies too. The person may still be breathing, but what they built together stops. And the one left behind carries a loss that has no coffin, no ceremony, no flowers on the porch.

Loss did not need to look the same to weigh the same.

❧

When Thomas stood to leave, the woman did not stop him.

"Come again," she said—not as invitation, not as expectation. Simply as fact.

He nodded.

At the door, he paused.

He wanted to say something—about what she had carried, about what it cost her to name it, about the strange mercy of contentment arriving only after everything else had been taken.

He didn't.

She already knew.

Outside, the mountain received him again, snow-muted and sure. The path back felt narrower now, but clearer. Each step pressed into the snow, leaving a mark that would fade by morning.

Thomas descended the ridge slowly, the village lights appearing below him one by one, small and warm in the early dark. The cold pressed against his face and he let it. His eyes were still damp. He did not wipe them.

Something had shifted—not in his chest, exactly. Somewhere lower. Somewhere more permanent. The weight he carried had not lifted.

It had been witnessed.

And for the first time, that felt like enough.

## When the Ice Began to Loosen

The change came subtly.

The shift arrived without announcement.

Days lengthened by minutes at a time. The light caught the upper slopes and warmed them just enough to soften the ice. Snow still fell, but it no longer settled with the same authority. It melted where it landed, leaving darkened ground in its place.

The village responded without comment.

Fires burned a little less. Paths widened. Doors stayed open longer in the mornings. No one spoke of spring. They did not need to.

Thomas felt the change in himself as well.

The grief remained—he had stopped expecting it to leave—but it no longer defined the shape of his days. It rose and fell now, like the mountain weather, something to be lived with rather than overcome.

He passed the locked church again one afternoon, its door reemerging from beneath snow, the arch wet and darkened by meltwater.

He stopped briefly.

Not to test it. Not to wait.

Only to acknowledge it.

Then he continued on.

The path did not require permission.

# The Way Home

The man was waiting at the edge of the village, as if he had known.

Thomas stopped a few paces away, his bag on his shoulder, the path ahead already beginning to widen.

They stood together for a moment, neither speaking. The morning light caught the mountains in pale gold. Aspens were budding. The air carried something it hadn't in months—warmth. Not much. Just enough to notice.

The man looked at him the way he always had—without evaluation, without expectation. Just presence.

"You'll carry it differently now," he said.

Thomas nodded. "I know."

The man was quiet for a moment. Then he said something Thomas didn't expect.

"I'm going back to her now," he said. "We take our walk in the mornings. She does better when the light is new."

Thomas felt the weight of it—not as sadness, but as something closer to reverence. This man would walk back to his cabin, lift his wife from the bed, dress her, hold her hand, and walk her along the same trail he had walked a thousand times. And he would do it tomorrow. And the day after. Not because she would know. Because he would.

"How do you see it?" Thomas asked. "What your life has become?"

The man considered the question.

"An honor," he said.

Thomas waited.

"I made a covenant," the man said. "In sickness and in health. I didn't know what that meant when I said it. I thought I did. I thought sickness meant a cold, a bad year, something we'd get through together. I didn't know it meant this. But the covenant doesn't change because the cost goes up. It means what it meant the day I said it."

He looked toward the trail that led to his cabin.

"My life is in service now," he said. "To her. To what I promised. To something larger than what I lost. And I give it willingly. Not because she asks—she can't ask. Because giving your life for the one you love is not a burden. It's the highest thing you can do."

Thomas felt the shape of something he couldn't name—something ancient and familiar, as if he had heard this story before in a different form, in a different voice, in a place he couldn't quite remember.

A man who gave everything for someone who couldn't fully receive it. Who forgave the unforgivable. Who chose love in the face of rejection. Who kept showing up, kept tending, kept holding the hand of someone who didn't know she was being held.

The guide touched the cord on his wrist—the one his daughter had tied there, the one that told him where home was.

"Go home," he said to Thomas. Not as a command. As a blessing.

Thomas extended his hand. The man took it—firmly, briefly—and then released it.

He turned and walked toward the trail without looking back. His steps were unhurried, measured, certain. The same pace he would use with his wife in an hour. The same patience. The same devotion.

Thomas watched him until the path curved and the trees received him.

Then he turned toward the road, the world opening ahead of him, the mountains rising behind—white and patient and sure.

He did not know the man's name.

He never would.

But he would carry the shape of him—the steady hands, the quiet voice, the cord on his wrist, the way he walked beside someone who could not walk alone—for the rest of his life.

# The Way Between

When he returned home, people noticed the difference.

They commented on it cautiously—his stillness, the way he listened more than he spoke. Someone asked him once what the mountains had given him.

Thomas considered the question.

"Space," he said.

That was all.

He walked more often now. Sat in silence without filling it. Let grief surface without naming it as something that needed to be solved. He carried his brother with him—not as absence, but as presence reshaped. Sometimes it was the laugh. Sometimes just the squint—that particular squint Daniel wore whenever he was turning something over in his mind, present and alive and still himself.

❧

One afternoon, Thomas walked through town.

Not toward anything. Just walking the way he had learned to walk on the mountain—without urgency, without destination, letting his steps follow whatever the ground offered.

A man walked past him carrying groceries, one bag slipping, his jaw set tight. Not from the weight of the bags. From the weight of whatever he was carrying home to.

A kid sat on a curb down the block, knees drawn up, head resting on his arms. Not sleeping. Just sitting with something too big for his body.

He passed a woman sitting alone at a bus stop. Her coat was buttoned one off, the kind of thing you'd only notice if you looked. A cup of coffee sat beside her on the bench, long cold. Her eyes moved across the street—not watching anything, just moving, the way eyes do when staying still means feeling too much.

Something in his chest tightened. Not sympathy. His body recognized the posture before his mind caught up.

As he passed, her eyes met his.

Thomas did not look away. He let her see him—his face, his eyes, the way his shoulders carried what they carried. Something she recognized. Something she had perhaps been looking for without knowing it.

"Do you have a moment?" she asked. Her voice was quiet. Not hopeful. Not even sure.

Thomas nodded. “I do.”

He sat down on the bench. Not close. Not far.

A bus came and went. She didn’t get on it. He didn’t move.

She looked at her hands. “My mother died three weeks ago.” Her voice was even, the way it sounds when a person has said something out loud in their head many times before saying it out loud in the world. “I keep reaching for the phone to tell her things. I haven’t gotten used to not calling yet.”

Thomas did not speak. He did not turn his body toward her. He simply stayed where he was, present to what she had placed between them.

“I don’t know why I told you that,” she said.

“You don’t have to know,” Thomas said.

She let out a breath she seemed not to have known she was holding.

They sat without speaking. The street moved around them. After a while, her hands, which had been clasped tight in her lap, loosened. Her shoulders settled.

When she stood, Thomas stood with her.

For a moment they simply faced each other. She was smaller than he had noticed while they sat—her coat loose on her shoulders, her eyes holding a tiredness that wasn't about sleep.

Then she stepped forward and put her arms around him.

Thomas returned the hug. He did not pat her back. He did not loosen his hold when the moment began to lengthen. He simply held her the way he had learned to hold everything now—steadily, without measuring, without asking it to be something else.

She held on a beat longer than strangers do.

When she finally pulled back, she did not step away. Her eyes met his, and she did not hurry to move. Thomas saw the tear on her cheek. She saw his. Neither of them wiped them away.

Then she picked up her bag, and she walked away.

He expected the bench to have taken something from him. Instead, he found no hollowing-out at all.

He had offered a stranger nothing he could measure—only his presence, only his willingness to remain—and somehow that had been enough. He thought of the guide, who walked beside someone every morning who could not walk alone—and never once seemed diminished by it. Thomas had wondered how. He understood now.

Not because he carried some hidden reserve. Not because grief had made him stronger. But because what moved through him was never his to manufacture.

Like breath, it came. Like breath, it went. And in the space left open by sorrow, more was given.

The breaking open, he realized, was not only the wound.

It was also the way in.

❧

Sometimes, when the world grew loud again, he remembered the way the path had narrowed, how snow had softened its edges, how doors had remained closed and yet he had not been turned away.

The memory did not instruct him.

It invited him.

Thomas understood now that the way had never belonged to the mountain.

It had always been within reach—between what was lost and what was still being given, between waiting and walking, between grief and hope.

He stepped into it again, each day, quietly.

And somewhere—unseen, unnamed—he was not walking alone.

# About the Author

Jerod Hurnblad is a nursing student at Joyce University of Nursing & Health Sciences, graduating as an RN in August 2026. He has worked the oncology and end-of-life floor at Asante Hospital in Medford, Oregon, and served on call at Celia's House—Southern Oregon's only residential nonprofit hospice—moving between both ends of the dying process by choice.

He chose to become a CNA first, deliberately, because he wanted to learn what care actually looks like before he was responsible for directing it. That decision gave him an intimate, ground-level view of what it means to be present with another human being at their most vulnerable.

He has been in recovery for twenty-five years and is a supporter and connector for Recovery Cafe Medford. He is married with three children, and their family has fostered eight children over the years. He lives in Medford, Oregon.

*The Way Between is his first book.*

jerodhurnblad.com

www.ingramcontent.com/pod-product-compliance
Lightning Source LLC
LaVergne TN
LVHW091813110826
845146LV00006B/1029